ADVENTURES IN THE SKIN TRADE

ALDINE PAPERBACKS

# Dylan Thomas

# ADVENTURES
## in the
# SKIN TRADE

*Foreword by*
VERNON WATKINS

J. M. DENT & SONS LTD

All rights reserved
Printed in Great Britain
by
Fletcher & Son Ltd · Harford Works · Norwich
for
J. M. DENT & SONS LTD
Aldine House · Bedford Street · London
First published by Putnam & Company Limited 1955
Paperback Edition 1965
Reprinted 1966, 1969

SBN: 460 02038 2

## Foreword

I was staying with Dylan Thomas in Laugharne early in 1941 when a letter arrived for which he had been waiting. It was from his publishers. He opened it eagerly, but the contents were disappointing. I do not remember the name of the publishers, but the letter made it clear that the manuscript he had sent them was not the great, serious autobiographical work to which they had been looking forward. They would be returning the manuscript and they would look forward to receiving something different at a later date.

We walked into the garden of Laugharne Castle, where Dylan often used to work at that time in the summer-house. He was indignant, and yet amused by the note. Why did publishers always want a writer to impress people, rather than to entertain them? His serious work, he knew, was in his poetry. His *Eighteen Poems*, *Twenty-five Poems* and the poems in *The Map of Love*, the book whose publication had almost coincided with

9

the outbreak of war, represented a particular progress, a casting-off of those habiliments which his newly baptised genius no longer needed. And in the last of these poems he had said:

> 'In the final direction of the elementary town
> I advance for as long as forever is.'

I had myself been a very intimate witness of that progress, for, although I did not meet Dylan until his first book had been published, I had been sent or shown every poem of the second book, and Dylan also sent me every poem in *The Map of Love*, just after it was written.

At the same time he showed me his stories, but the progress of these was different. The very first story he read to me was *The Orchards*. This was the story in which his Joycean Welsh place-name Llareggub first appeared, the name which was to be the provisional title much later of *Under Milk Wood*. There occurred also in this story the phrase 'a desireless familiar' which he was after-wards to use in the poem in *Deaths and Entrances* with the title "To Others Than You". There was indeed a connection between the stories and the poems, but it was soon to be broken. He suddenly abandoned the highly charged, artificial yet impulsive symbolism of such stories as *The Orchards*,

*The Lemon* and the unfinished fragment *In The Direction of The Beginning* at about the time of his twenty-fourth birthday, when the birthday poem which I have quoted was written. Quite suddenly he began to write about people as they actually were and behaved. Through the exact memory he had of his childhood and an extraordinary power to recreate it he released a spring of comedy, both of character and situation, which had been hidden from himself because it was at first too close to his experience. These were the stories about Swansea and the surroundings of that, his native town; and very Welsh they were, more true to Swansea than Swansea itself. He collected them in 1940 under the title *Portrait of the Artist as a Young Dog.*

It was after these stories that Dylan began to turn over in his head another that he wanted to write. It would be an extended story, not strictly autobiographical, but bearing a relation to the two parts of his experience, his own actions and the actions of his dramatised self. What he did figuratively the central character of the story would do in real life, and he would take the very train from his parents' home to unknown London which Dylan took.

This story was in a certain way most ambitious, at least as it was first planned. The central character, Samuel Bennet, would attract adventures to him by his own unadventurous stillness and natural acceptance of every situation. He would accept life in every position, like a baby who had been given self-dependence. He would have no money, no possessions, no extra clothes, no civilised bias. And life would come to him. People would come, and they would bring him life. Odd, very odd people would come. But whoever came, and whatever situation came, he would go on. Then, at a certain point, an unpredictable point in time, he would look back and find that he had shed a skin.

In Dylan's first plan, so far as I can remember it, there were to be seven skins. At the end of the story the character would be naked at last. It would be in one way a journey through the Inferno of London, but it would also be a comedy.

Dylan read me the first chapters, certainly the first two. He was still undecided about a title and we discussed possible titles. *The Skins* was not quite right. *A Trader in Skins* or *A Traveller in Skins* might do. Then, from the big house near Chippenham where he was staying with John Davenport, he wrote that he was going for long bicycle rides and thinking of his story to be called *Adventures in the Skin Trade*.

Towards the end of May he was back in Laugharne Castle, and he wrote: "My prosebook's going well, but I dislike it. It's the only really dashed-off piece of work I remember doing. I've done 10,000 words already. It's indecent and trivial, sometimes funny, sometimes mawkish, and always badly written which I do not mind so much." This was a characteristically modest statement, an underrating of what he was doing.

A week later came a more amplified statement: "My novel blathers on. It's a mixture of Oliver Twist, Little Dorrit, Kafka, Beachcomber, and good old 3-adjectives-a-penny belly-churning Thomas, the Rimbaud of Cwmdonkin Drive."

Dylan was at this time hard up. It must have been soon after this that I went down to see him in Laugharne and the disappointing letter from the publishers arrived. I do not know how many chapters he had sent them, but he very soon dismissed the letter and continued work on the book. He disappeared in the afternoon, and showed me a new part he had written when he emerged for tea. It covered about a page and was extremely funny. He wrote this kind of prose and dialogue quickly, like the *Portrait of the Artist* stories. Then he would revise what he had written. This method stood in sharp contrast to the composition of his poetry in which he used separate work-sheets and built the poem up, phrase by phrase, at glacier-like speed.

Since composition of this comic kind of writing came so easily to Dylan, and since it exercised his gift for entertaining others and interesting himself at the same time, it may be wondered why he stopped after writing four chapters. A possible reason is that he distrusted his own facility. A more likely reason is, I think, the impact of war, and particularly of the London air raids, on his appalled and essentially tragic vision. He was able to reconstruct out of joy the truth of his child-hood, both in his poems and in his broadcast scripts, for those experiences were real; but what was only half real, half fictional, he had to abandon.

The first chapter of *Adventures in the Skin Trade*, "A Fine Beginning", was printed in Mr. John Lehmann's Folios of New Writing V in the Autumn of 1941. It was reprinted in the United States early in 1953 in the Second Mentor Book of *New World Writing*, with the second chapter; and the third and fourth, entitled "Four Lost Souls", were printed in the Third Mentor Book in May of the same year. At the end of the year the first two chapters were printed in the Dylan Thomas Memorial number of *Adam*.

Although these chapters have been printed separately, it is remarkable that they have not until now been published as a book. Like everything Dylan wrote, and like all the rich comedy found in his letters or remembered in his conversation, this unique fragment carries the stamp of his personality. It is real now because it was once real to him; it is alive because it was once a part of his own life, and because it holds the key to a certain attitude to the world and to situation which was peculiarly his own. This attitude, which may be defined as a rooted opposition to material progress, he continued to hold long after he had abandoned work on the novel. Its anarchic fantasy appealed to him, and it is one more example of the poet's indifference to reputation, of his refusal to follow the advance guard of his fame. Had circumstances been different he would have continued it, for it was a theme which had occupied him intensively for a year, perhaps two, and which continued to haunt him as late as June, 1953, when, in a letter to Oscar Williams, he wrote that he would "begin to go on with the Adventures in the Skin Trade". As it was, at the time when he stopped writing these pages, the pressure of the anarchy of war itself and the vision of distorted London took the place of his half-fictional vision and compelled his imagination forward to the "Ceremony After A Fire Raid", and to the beautiful poems evoking childhood, "It Was My Thirtieth Year To Heaven" and "Fern Hill". He could still go back to peace, but from there he could no longer go forward. Something had happened which prevented him from making the journey Samuel Bennet made, and which he himself had made ten years before.

VERNON WATKINS

*May* 1955

# I

# *A Fine Beginning*

## I

THAT EARLY morning, in January 1933, only one
person was awake in the street, and he was the
quietest. Call him Samuel Bennet. He wore a
trilby hat that had been lying by his bedside in
case the two house-breakers, a man and a woman,
came back for the bag they had left.

In striped pyjamas tight under the arms and
torn between the legs, he padded barefoot downstairs and opened the breakfast-room door of his
parents' six-room house. The room smelt strong
of his father's last pipe before bed. The windows
were shut fast and the curtains drawn, the back
door was bolted, the house-breaking night could
not enter anywhere. At first he peered uneasily
into the known, flickering corners of the room, as
though he feared that the family might have been
sitting there in silence in the dark; then he lit the
gaslight from the candle. His eyes were still heavy
from a dream of untouchable city women and

falling, but he could see that Tinker, the aunt-faced pom, was sleeping before the burned-out fire, and that the mantelpiece clock between hollow, mock-ebony, pawing horses, showed five to two. He stood still and listened to the noises of the house: there was nothing to fear. Upstairs the family breathed and snored securely. He heard his sister sleeping in the box-room under the signed photographs of actors from the repertory theatre and the jealous pictures of the marriages of friends. In the biggest bedroom overlooking the field that was called the back, his father turned over the bills of the month in his one dream; his mother in bed mopped and polished through a wood of kitchens. He closed the door: now there was nobody to disturb him.

But all the noises of the otherwise dead or sleeping, dark early morning, the intimate breathing of three invisible relations, the loud old dog, could wake up the neighbours. And the gaslight, bubbling, could attract to his presence in the breakfast-room at this hour Mrs. Probert next door, disguised as a she-goat in a nightgown, butting the air with her kirby-grips; her dapper, commercial son, with a watch-chain tattooed across his rising belly; the tubercular lodger, with his neat umbrella up and his basin in his hand. The regular tide of the family breath could beat against the wall of the house on the other side, and bring the Baxters out. He turned the gas low and stood for a minute by the clock, listening to sleep and seeing Mrs. Baxter climb naked out of her widow's bed with a mourning band round her thigh.

Soon her picture died, she crawled back grieving to her lovebird's mirror under the blankets, and the proper objects of the room slowly returned as he lost his fear that the strangers upstairs he had known since he could remember would wake and come down with pokers and candles.

First there was the long strip of snapshots of his mother propped against the cut-glass of the window-sill. A professional under a dickybird hood had snapped her as she walked down Chapel Street in December, and developed the photographs while she waited looking at the thermos flasks and the smoking sets in the nearest shop-window, calling "Good morning" across the street to the shopping bags she knew, and the matron's outside costumes, and the hats like flower-pots and chambers on the crisp, permed heads. There she was, walking down the street along the window-sill, step by step, stout, safe, confident, buried in her errands, clutching her handbag, stepping aside from the common women blind and heavy under a week's provisions,

prying into the looking-glasses at the doors of
furniture shops.

"Your photograph has been taken." Immor-
talized in a moment, she shopped along forever
between the cut-glass vase with the permanent
flowers and the box of hairpins, buttons, screws,
empty shampoo packets, cotton-reels, flypapers,
cigarette cards. At nearly two in the morning she
hurried down Chapel Street against a backcloth of
trilbies and Burberries going the other way, umbrellas rising to the first drops of the rain a month
ago, the sightless faces of people who would always
be strangers hanging half-developed behind her,
and the shadows of the shopping centre of the
sprawling, submerged town. He could hear her
shoes click on the tramrails. He could see, beneath
the pastelled silk scarf, the round metal badge of
Mrs. Rosser's Society, and the grandmother's
cameo brooch on the vee of the knitted clover
jumper.

The clock chimed and struck two. Samuel put
out his hand and took up the strip of snaps. Then
he tore it into pieces. The whole of her dead, comfortable face remained on one piece, and he tore it
across the cheeks, up through the chins, and into
the eyes.

The pom growled in a nightmare, and showed

his little teeth. "Lie down, Tinker. Go to sleep, boy." He put the pieces in his pyjama pocket.

Then there was the framed photograph of his sister by the clock. He destroyed her in one movement, and, with the ripping of her set smile and the crumpling of her bobbed head into a ball, down went the Girls' School and the long-legged, smiling colts with their black knickers and bows; the hockey-legged girls who laughed behind their hands as they came running through the gates when he passed, went torn and ruined into his pyjama pocket; they vanished, broken, into the porch and lay in pieces against his heart. Stanley Road, where the Girls' School stood, would never know him again. Down you go, Peggy, he whispered to his sister, with all the long legs and the Young Liberals' dances, and the boys you brought home for supper on Sunday evenings and Lionel you kissed in the porch. He is a solicitor now. When I was eleven years old and you were seventeen I heard you, from my bedroom, playing the Desert Song. People were downstairs all over the world.

Most of the history sheets on the table were already marked and damned in his father's violet writing. With a lump of coal from the dead fire, Samuel marked them again, rubbing the coal hard over the careful corrections, drawing legs and breasts in the margins, smudging out the names and form numbers. History is lies. Now take Queen Elizabeth. Go ahead, take Alice Phillips, take her into the shrubbery. She was the headmaster's daughter. Take old Bennet and whip him down the corridors, stuff his mouth with dates, dip his starched collar in his marking ink and hammer his teeth back into his prim, bald, boring head with his rap-across-the-knuckle ruler. Spin Mr. Nicholson on his tellurion until his tail drops off. Tell Mr. Parsons his wife has been seen coming out of the Compass piggyback on a drunk sailor, catching pennies in her garters. It's as true as History.

On the last sheet he signed his name several times under a giant pinman with three legs. He did not scribble on the top sheet. At a first glance there was no sign of interference. Then he threw the coal into the grate. Dust drifted up in a cloud, and settled down again on the pom's back.

If only he could shout at the ceiling now, at the dark circle made by the gas, at the cracks and lines that had always been the same faces and figures, two bearded men chasing an animal over a mountain edge, a kneeling woman with faces on her knees: Come and look at Samuel Bennet destroying his parents' house in Mortimer Street, off

Stanley's Grove; he will never be allowed to come back. Mrs. Baxter, have a dekko from under the cold sheets: Mr. Baxter, who worked in the Harbour Trust Office, can never come back either. Mrs. Probert Chestnuts, your billygoat is gone, leaving a hairy space in the bed; Mr. Bell the lodger coughs all night under his gamp; your son cannot sleep, he is counting his gentlemen's three and eleven-three half-hose jumping over the tossed blankets. Samuel shouted under his breath, "Come and see me destroying the evidence, Mrs. Rosser; have a peep from under your hairnet. I have seen your shadow on the blind as you undressed, I was watching by the lamp-post next to the dairy; you disappeared under a tent and came out slim and humped and black. I am the only gooseberry in Stanley's Grove who knows that you are a black woman with a hump. Mr. Rosser married to a camel; every one is mad and bad in his box when the blinds are pulled; come and see me break the china without any noise so that I can never come back."

"Hush," he said to himself, "I know you."

He opened the door of the china pantry. The best plates shone in rows, a willow tree next to an ivied castle, baskets of solid flowers on top of fruits and flower-coiled texts. Tureens were piled on one shelf, on another the salad-bowls, the finger-bowls, the toast-racks spelling Porthcawl and Baby, the trifle-dishes, the heirloom moustache-cup. The afternoon tea-service was brittle as biscuits and had gold rims. He cracked two saucers together, and the horn-curved spout of the teapot came off in his hand. In five minutes he had broken the whole set. Let all the daughters of Mortimer Street come in and see me, he whispered in the close pantry: the pale young girls who help at home, calculating down the pavement to the rich-smelling shops, screwing up their straight, dry hair in their rooms at the top of the house; their blood is running through them like salt. And I hope the office girls knock on the door with the stubs of their fingers, tap out Sir or Madam on the glass porch, the hard, bright babies who never go too far. You can hear them in the lane behind the post office as you tiptoe along, they are saying, "So he said and I said and he said and Oh yeah I said," and the just male voices are agreeing softly. Shoo them in out of snoring Stanley's Grove, I know they are sleeping under the sheets up to their fringes in wishes. Beryl Gee is marrying the Chamber of Commerce in a pepper-and-salt church. Mrs. Mayor's Chain, Madame Cocked Hat, Lady Settee, I am breaking tureens in the cupboard under the stairs.

A tureen-cover dropped from his hand and smashed.

He waited for the sound of his mother waking. No one stirred upstairs. "Tinker did it," he said aloud, but the harsh noise of his voice drove him back into silence. His fingers became so cold and numb he knew he could not lift up another plate to break it.

"What are you doing?" he said to himself at last, in a cool, flat voice. "Leave the Street alone. Let it sleep."

Then he closed the pantry door.

"What are you doing, ranting away?"

Even the dog had not been wakened.

"Ranting away," he said.

He would have to be quick now. The accident in the cupboard had made him tremble so much that he could hardly tear up the bills he found in the sideboard drawer and scatter them under the sofa. His sister's crochet-work was too difficult to destroy, the doilies and the patterned tea-cosies were hard as rubber. He pulled them apart the best he could, and wedged them up the chimney.

"These are such small things," he said. "I should break the windows and stuff the cushions with the glass." He saw his round soft face in the mirror under the Mona Lisa. "But you won't," he

said, turning away; "you're afraid of the noise."
He turned back to his reflection. "It isn't that.
You're afraid she'll cut her hands."

He burnt the edge of his mother's sunshade at
the gas-mantle, and felt the tears running down his
cheeks and dropping on to his pyjama collar.

Even in the first moment of his guilt and shame,
he remembered to put out his tongue and taste the
track of the tears. Still crying, he said, "It's salt.
It's very salt. Just like in my poems."

He went upstairs in the dark, with the candle
shaking, past the box-room to his own room, and
locked the door on the inside. He put out his hands
and touched the walls and his bed. Good morning
and good-bye, Mrs. Baxter. His window, facing
her bedroom, was open to the windless, starless
early morning, but he could not hear her breathe or
sleep. All the houses were quiet. The street was a
close grave. The Rossers and the Proberts and the
Bennets were still and safe and deep in their separate silences. His head touched the pillow, but he
knew that he could not sleep again. His eyes
closed.

Come down into my arms, for I shan't sleep,
girls asleep on all sides in the attics and spare rooms
of the square, red houses with the bay windows
looking out on the trees behind the railings. I

know your rooms like the backs of my hands, like the backs of your heads in the pictures when you are leaning over on to the next-door shoulders. I shan't sleep again. Tomorrow, today, I am going away by the 7.15 train, with ten pounds and a new suit-case. Lay your curling-pins on my pillow, the alarm at six-thirty will hurry you back to draw the blinds and light the fires before the rest come down. Come down quickly, the Bennets' house is melting. I can hear you breathe, I can hear Mrs. Baxter turn in a dream. Oh, the milk-men are waking!

He was asleep with his hat on still, and his hands clenched.

2

THE FAMILY awoke before six o'clock. He heard them, from a sunken half-sleep, bothering on the landing. They would be in dressing-gowns, stale-eyed and with ragged hair. Peggy might have put two blushes on her cheeks. The family rushed in and out of the bathroom, never stopping to wash, and collided on the narrow top of the stairs as they nagged and bustled to get him ready. He let himself sink deeper until the waves broke round his head again, and the lights of a city spun and shone through the eyes of women walking in his last remembered dream. From the lapping distance he heard his father shout like a man on the opposite shore:

"Have you put the sponge bag in, Hilda?"

"Of course I have," she answered from the kitchen.

Don't let her look in the china-pantry, Samuel prayed among the women walking like lamp-posts. She never uses the best china for breakfast.

"All right, all right; I just asked."

"Where's his new hairbrush?"

"That's right, shout my head off. Here it is. How can I give it to you if you're in the kitchen? It's the brush with the initials—S.B."

"I know his initials."

"Mother, does he want all these vests? You know he never uses them."

"It's January, Peggy."

"She knows it's January, Hilda. You haven't got to tell the neighbours. Can you smell something burning?"

"It's only mother's sunshade," Samuel said in the locked bedroom.

He dressed and went down. The gas in the breakfast-room was on again. His mother was boiling an egg for him on the gas-stove. "We'll have our breakfast later," she said; "you mustn't miss the train. Did you sleep well?"

"No burglars last night, Sam," his father said.

His mother brought the egg in. "You can't expect them every night."

Peggy and his father sat down in front of the empty grate.

"What do you think you'll do first when you get there, Sam?" said Peggy.

"He'll get himself a nice room, of course, not too central. And don't have an Irish landlady." His mother brushed his collar as he ate. "Go and get yourself settled straight away; that's the important thing."

"I'll get myself settled."

"Don't forget to look under the wallpaper for bugs."

"That's enough of that, Peggy. Sam knows a clean place when he sees one."

He saw himself knocking at a lodging-house in the very centre of the city, and an Irishwoman appearing at the door. "Good morning, madam. Have you a cheap room?" "Cheaper than sunlight to you, Danny Boy." She would not be more than twenty-one. "Has it got bugs?" "All over the walls, praise be to God." "I'll take it."

"I'll know what I'm doing," he said to his mother.

"Jenkins' motor isn't here yet," Peggy said. "Perhaps there's a puncture."

If he doesn't come soon, they'll notice everything. I'll cut my throat on a piece of china.

"Remember to call on Mrs. Chapman. Give her all our love from 42."

"I'll call on her tomorrow, mother."

The taxi drew up outside. The corners of bedroom blinds would be lifted all over the street.

"Here's your wallet. Don't put it in your handkerchief pocket now. You never know when you'll be wanting to blow your nose."

"You'll be scattering largesse," Peggy said. She kissed him on the forehead.

Remind me to wipe it off in the cab.

"You're kissing the editor of the *Times* now," said his mother.

"Well, not quite that, Sam. Not yet, eh?" His father said, "Rungs of the ladder," and then looked away.

"Write tomorrow morning sharp. Send us the news."

"You send me your news, too. Mr. Jenkins is blowing his horn."

"Better than blowing your trumpet," Peggy said. "And there's never any news in Mortimer Street."

You wait, slyboots. Wait till the flames touch the doilie with the herons on it.

He came down to pat Tinker.

"Come on, don't fuss over the old dog; he's all fleas. It's gone seven."

Peggy was opening the door of the taxi for him. His father shook him by the hand. His mother kissed him on the mouth.

"Good-bye, Mortimer Street," he said, and the cab was off. "Good-bye, Stanley's Grove."

Through the back window he saw three strangers waving. He pulled down the blind.

3

SITTING WITH his bag in the lavatory of the moving train, for all the compartments were full, he read through his notebook and tore out the pages in order. He was dressed in a brand-new brown

tweed overcoat, a brown town-suit, a white
starched shirt with a woollen tie and a tiepin, and
black, shining shoes. He had put his hard brown
hat in the wash-basin. Here was Mrs. Chapman's
address next to the telephone number of a Mr.
Hewson who was going to introduce him to a man
who worked on a newspaper; and under these the
address of the Literary Institute that had once
awarded him a guinea for a poem in a competition:
Will Shakespeare at the Tomb of the Unknown
Warrior. He tore the page out. Then the name
and address, in red ink, of a collected poet who had
written him a letter thanking him for a sonnet-
sequence. And a page of names that might help.

The lavatory door half opened, and he shut it
quickly with his foot.

"I beg your pardon."

Hear her apologizing down the corridor, full as
an egg. She could turn every handle the whole
length of the train, and in every closet a fully-
clothed man would be sitting with his foot against
the door, lost and alone in the long, moving house
on wheels, travelling in silence with no windows, at
sixty miles an hour racing to another place that did
not want him, never at home wherever the train
stopped. The handle turned again, and Samuel
coughed somebody away.

The last page of the notebook was the only one he kept. Under a drawing of a girl with long hair dancing into an address, he had written: Lucille Harris. A man he met on the Promenade had said as they sat on a bench, looking at the legs passing: "She's okay. She's a girl I know. She's the best in the world; she'll take care of you. Give her a call when you're up. Tell her you're Austin's friend." That page he placed in his wallet between two one-pound notes.

The rest of the pages he picked up from the floor, bunched together, and threw down between his legs into the bowl. Then he pulled the chain. Down went the helping names the influential numbers, the addresses that could mean so much, into the round, roaring sea and on to the rails. Already they were lost a mile behind, blowing over the track now, over the glimpses of hedges into the lightning-passing fields.

Home and help were over. He had eight pounds ten and Lucille Harris' address. Many people have begun worse, he said aloud. I am ignorant, lazy, dishonest, and sentimental; I have the pull over nobody.

The handle turned again.

"I bet you're dancing," he said to the person the other side of the locked door.

Footsteps pattered away down the train.

First of all, when I reach there, I'll have a Bass and a stale sandwich, he decided. I'll take them to a table in a corner, brush off the cakecrumbs with my hat, and prop my book against the cruet. I must have all the details right at the beginning. The rest must come by accident. I'll be sitting there before noon, cool and calm, my hat on my knees, my glass in my hand, looking not a day under twenty, pretending to read and spying from the corners of my eyes at the waiting, drinking, restless people busily alone at the counter. The other tables will be crowded. There will be women, beckoning without moving, over their cold coffee; old, anonymous men with snuff on their cheeks, trembling over tea; quiet men expecting no one from the trains they wait for eagerly every hour; women who have come to run away, to take a train to St. Ives or Liverpool or anywhere, but who know they will never take any train and are drinking cups of tea and saying to themselves, "I could be catching the twelve o'clock but I'll wait for the quarter past"; women from the country with dozens of children coming undone; shop girls, office girls, street girls, people who have nothing worse to do, all the unhappy, happy in chains, bewildered foreign men and women in the station buffet of the city I know from cover to cover.

The door rattled. "You there," a voice said outside. "You've been there for hours."

He turned on the hot-water tap. It spurted cold water into the basin before he could take his hat out. "I'm a director of the company," he said, but his voice sounded weak to him and without assurance.

When the footsteps had faded again, he gathered up his cases and walked out of the lavatory and down the corridor. Standing outside a first-class compartment, he saw a man and a ticket-inspector come to the door and hammer on it. They did not try the handle.

"Ever since Neath," the man said.

Now the train was losing speed, running out of the lost country into the smoke and a tunnel of factories, puffing past the district platforms and the high houses with broken windows and underclothes dancing in the dirty yards. Children at the windows never waved their hands to the train. It might have been the wind passing.

A crowd of people stood arguing outside the door as the train drew up under a great glass roof.

4

"Nip of Bass, please, and a ham sandwich." He took them to a table in a corner, brushed off the crumbs with his wet hat, and sat down just before noon. He counted his money: eight pound nine and a penny, nearly three pounds more than he had ever seen. Some people had this every week. It had to last him until he was dead. At the next table sat a plump, middle-aged man with a chocolate-brown birthmark over his cheek and chin like the half of a beard. He was propping his book against an empty bottle when a young man walked over from the counter.

"Hullo, Sam."

"Hullo, Ron. Fancy seeing you."

He was Ronald Bishop who used to live in the Crescent off Stanley's Grove.

"Been up in the smoke for long, Sam?"

"Just arrived. How's tricks?"

"Same as me, we must have been on the same train. Oh, so so. Still at the old game, Sam?"

"Yeah, up on a bit of business. You at the usual?"

"Yeah."

They had never had anything to say to each other.

"Where you staying, Ron?"

"Usual. Strand Palace."

"Daresay I'll be seeing you, then."

"Okay, make it tomorrow in the bar, about seven-thirty."

"Okay."

"It's a date, don't forget."

"No fear."

They both forgot it at once.

"Well, be seeing you."

"Be good."

As Ronald Bishop walked off, Samuel said silently into his glass: A fine beginning. If I go out of the station and turn round the corner I'll be back in 42. The little Proberts will be playing doctor outside the Load of Hay. The only stranger anywhere near me is a business-man with a stained face, reading the palms of his hands. No, here comes a woman in a fur coat; she's going to sit next to me. Yes, no, no. I smelt her as she passed; eau-de-Cologne and powder and bed.

The woman sat down two tables away, crossed her legs, powdered her nose.

This is the beginning of an advance. Now she is

pretending not to notice that her knees are un-
covered. There's a lynx in the room, lady. Button
your overcoat. She's rattling her spoon on her
saucer to attract my attention, but when I stare at
her hard, without smiling, I see she is looking down
gently and innocently into her lap as though she
had a baby there. He was glad she was not brazen.

Dear mother, he wrote with his finger on the
back of an envelope, looking up, between every
few invisible words, at the unnoticing woman opposite, this is to tell you that I arrived safely and
that I am drinking in the buffet with a tart. I will
tell you later if she is Irish. She is about thirty-
eight years old and her husband left her five years
ago because of her carryings on. Her child is in a
home, and she visits him every other Sunday. She
always tells him that she is working in a hat shop.
You need not worry that she will take all my money
as we liked each other on first sight. And you
need not worry that I shall break my heart trying
to reform her, because I have always been brought
up to believe that Mortimer Street is what is right,
and I would not wish that on anybody. Besides, I
do not want to reform her. Not that I think she is
nasty. Her business is very hard on stockings, so
I am going to pay the first week's rent for our little
room in Pimlico. Now she is going across to the

counter to buy another cup of coffee. I hope you will notice that she is buying her own. Everybody in the buffet is unhappy except me.

As she came back to her table, he tore up the envelope and stared at her, unsmiling, for a full minute by the Bovril clock. Once she raised her eyes to his, then looked away. She was tapping her spoon on the side of her cup, then opening and closing the clasp of her handbag, then turning her head round slowly to face him and then looking away again quickly through the window. She must be new, he thought with a sudden compassion, but he did not stop staring. Should I wink? He tilted his hard, wet hat over one eye, and winked: a long, deliberate wink that screwed up his face and made his burning cigarette nearly touch the blunt end of his nose. She snapped her handbag, pushed two pennies under the saucer, and walked right out of the room, never looking at him as she passed.

She's left her coffee, he thought. And then: My God, she was blushing.

A fine beginning.

"Did you speak?" asked the man with the birth-mark, spying up. His face was red and purple where it was not brown, faintly shabby and un-shaved, shiftily angry about the eyes as though his cunning were an irritation impossible to bear.

"I think I said it was a fine day."

"Stranger in town?"

"Yes, I've just come up."

"How do you like it?" He did not appear to care at all.

"I haven't been outside the station yet."

Now the woman in the fur coat would be telling a policeman, "I have just been winked at by a short boy wearing a wet hat." "But it isn't raining, madam." That would settle her.

He put his hat under the table.

"There's plenty to see," the man said, "if that's what you want. Museums, art galleries." Without speaking, he went through a list of names of other attractions, but rejected them all. "Museums," he said after a long pause. "There's one at South Kensington, and there's the British Museum, and there's one at Whitehall with guns. I've seen them all," he said.

Now every table was occupied. Cold, stiff people with time to kill sat staring at their tea and the clock, inventing replies to questions that would not be asked, justifying their behaviour in the past and the future, drowning every present moment as soon as it began to breathe, lying and wishing, missing all the trains in the terror of their minds, each one alone at the terminus. Time was dying all over the room. And then all the tables except the one next to Samuel's were unoccupied again. The lonely crowd went out in a funeral procession, leaving ash and tea-leaves and newspapers.

"You must move out of the station some time, you know," the man said, returning to a conversation that held no interest for him. "If you want to see around. It's only fair. It's not fair to come up in a train and sit in the buffet and then go back and say you've seen London, is it?"

"I'm going out now, quite soon."

"That's right," the man said, "give London a chance."

He is so tired of talking to me that he is nearly losing his temper, Samuel thought.

He looked around him again, at the mourners fidgeting to the counter, at the quick whisky drinkers in a knot by the tea-urn, at the waitresses listlessly busy with cardboard cakes and small change.

"Otherwise, it's like not getting out of bed, isn't it?" the man said. "You've got to walk round, you know, you've got to move some time. Everybody does it," he said in a sudden, dull passion.

Samuel bought another nip of Bass from a girl like Joan Crawford.

"This is the last one, then I'm going," he said when he had returned to his table.

"Do you think I care how many more you have?
You can stay here all day, why should I mind?"
The man was looking at the palms of his hands
again as his temper mounted. "Am I my brother's
keeper?"

Ronald Bishop still stood at the counter.

Mortimer Street has tracked me down, Samuel
thought bitterly, even into this lopsided quarrel
with a palmist in a station restaurant. There was
no escape. But it was not escape he wanted. The
Street was a safe hole in a wall behind the wind in
another country. He wanted to arrive and be
caught. Ronald stood there like a fury with a
rolled umbrella. Come in, Mrs. Rosser, in your
fawn and beige antimacassar coat, with your tribal
hat on your waves, and scream the news of the
Street across the table in your whist-drive voice. I
could not escape your fury on a birds' rock, you
would be mincing and pinching down to the fishy
sea with your beak gaped open like a shopping
bag.

"I hate a nosey parker," the man said, and got
up. On his way to the counter he passed the table
where the Irish prostitute had sat and removed the
pennies from under the plate.

"Stop, thief!" Samuel said softly. No one could
hear. There is a waitress with a consumptive hus-

band who needs those pennies. And two children, Tristram and Eve. He changed the names quickly. Tom and Marge. Then he walked over and put a sixpence under the plate just as a waitress came to the table.

"It fell on the floor," he said.

"Oh yeah?"

As he walked back, he saw that the waitress was talking to three men at the counter and nodding her head in his direction. One man was Ronald Bishop. One was the man with the birthmark.

Oh, fine, fine! If he had not broken the china he would have caught the next train back. The pieces would be swept up by now, but the tears would be running all over the house. "Mother, mother, he's put my crochet-work up the chimney," he heard his sister scream in a guard's whistle. Herons, flower baskets, palm trees, windmills, Red Riding Hoods, stuffed up in the flames and soot. "Get me a rubber to rub out coal, Hilda. I shall of course lose my position. That is only to be expected." "Oh my teapot, oh my blue set, oh my poor boy." He refused to look at the counter where Ronald Bishop inaudibly reviled him. The waitress knew as soon as she saw him that he stole from the begging tins of the blind and led them by the arm into thick traffic. The birthmarked man said that he had shown a certain postcard to a customer in a fur coat. The voices of his parents condemned above the clattering of the cups. He stared hard at his book though the print climbed and staggered as if the tears of the left house had run down after him along the rails and flowed into this hot, suspicious room over the tea-stained air into his eyes. But the image was false and the book was chosen for strangers. He did not like or understand it.

"My bills." "My doilies." "My willow-plate."

Ronald Bishop went out on to the platform.

"Be seeing you, Ron."

Ronald Bishop's face was flushed with the embarrassment of not noticing him.

One pleasure is, Samuel said to himself, that I do not know what I expect to happen to me. He smiled at the waitress behind the counter, and she stared away at once as guiltily as though he had discovered her robbing the till. I am not so innocent as I make out, he thought. I do not expect any old cobwebbed Fagin, reeking of character and stories, to shuffle out of a corner and lead me away into his grand, loud, filthy house; there will not be any Nancy to tickle my fancy in a kitchen full of handkerchiefs and beckoning, unmade beds. I did not think a choir of loose women immediately would sing and dance around the little tables, in plush cloths and advertised brassieres, as I walked into London for the first time, rattling my fortune, fresh as Copperfield. I could count the straws in my hair with one hand.

Hush! I know you, he said, cheater at Patience, keyhole peeper, keeper of nail-clippings and ear-wax, lusting after silhouettes on Laburnum's blind, searching for thighs in the Library of Classical Favourites, Sam Thumb in the manhole prying up on windy days.

I am not like that at all, he said, as the man with the birthmark came over to his table and sat down opposite him.

"I thought you were going," the man said. "You told me you were going. You've been here an hour now."

"I saw you," Samuel said.

"I know you saw me. You must have seen me, mustn't you, because you were looking at me," the man said. "Not that I want the twopence, I've got a house full of furniture. Three rooms full to the ceiling. I've got enough chairs for everyone in Paddington to have a sit down. Twopence is twopence," he said.

"But it was twopence to the waitress, too."

"She's got sixpence now, hasn't she? She's

made fourpence clear. It doesn't do any harm to you just because she thinks you were trying to nip it off her."

"It was my sixpence."

The man raised his hands. The palms were covered with calculations in ink. "And they talk about equality. Does it matter whose sixpence it was? It might have been mine or anybody's. There was talk of calling the manageress," he said, "but I put my foot down there."

They were both silent for several minutes.

"Made up your mind where you're going when you move out of here?" the man said at last. "Because move you must, some time, you know."

"I don't know where I'm going. I haven't any idea in the world. That's why I came up to London."

"Look here," the man said, controlling his voice, "there's sense in everything. There's bound to be. Otherwise we wouldn't be able to carry on, would we? Everybody knows where he's going, especially if he's come by train. Otherwise he wouldn't move from where he took the train from. That's elementary."

"People run away."

"Have you run away?"

"No."

"Then don't say it. Don't say it." His voice trembled; he looked at the figures on his palms. Then gently and patiently he began again. "Let's get the first thing straight. People who have come must go. People must know where they're going, otherwise the world could not be conducted on a sane basis. The streets would be full of people just wandering about, wouldn't they? Wandering about and having useless arguments with people who know where they're going. My name is Allingham, I live in Sewell Street off Praed Street, and I'm a furniture dealer. That's simple, isn't it? There's no need to complicate things if you keep your head and know who you are."

"I'm Samuel Bennet. I don't live anywhere at all. I don't do any work, either."

"Where are you going to go, then? I'm not a nosey parker, I told you my business."

"I don't know."

"He doesn't know," Mr. Allingham said. "Don't think you're anywhere now, mind. You can't call this place anywhere, can you? It's breathing space."

"I've been wondering what was going to happen. That's what I've been discussing with myself. I came up really to see what would happen to me. I don't want to make anything happen myself."

"He was discussing it with himself. With a boy
of twenty. How old are you?"

"Twenty."

"That's right. Discussing a question like that
with a boy just out of his teens. What did you expect to happen?"

"I don't know. Perhaps people would come up
and talk to me at the beginning. Women,"
Samuel said.

"Why should they talk to you? Why should I
talk to you? You're not going anywhere. You're
not doing anything. You don't exist," he said.

But all Samuel's strength was in his belly and
his eyes. He should veil his eyes or the marble-
topped counter might melt and all the clothes of
the girls behind them peel away and all the cups
chip on the shelves.

"Anyone might come up," he said. Then he
thought of his fine beginning. "Anyone," he said
without hope.

A clerk from the Crescent a dozen doors away;
a cold, ordinary woman from Birmingham, driven
off by a wink; anybody, anybody; a deacon from
the Valleys on a mean blind, with his pocket-book
sewn in his combs; an elderly female assistant on
holiday from a flannel and calico shop where the
change hums on wires. Nobody he had ever wanted.

"Oh, anyone of course. Janet Gaynor," Mr. Allingham said. "Marion Davies and Kay Francis and . . ."

"You don't understand. I don't expect that kind of person. I don't know what I do expect at all, but it isn't that."

"Modest."

"No, I'm not modest either. I don't believe in modesty. It's just that here I am and I don't know where to go. I don't want to know where to go."

Mr. Allingham began to plead, leaning across the table, pulling softly at Samuel's collar, showing the sums on his hands. "Don't say you don't want to know where to go. Please. There's a good boy. We must take things easy, mustn't we? We mustn't complicate things. Take one simple question. Now don't rush it. Take your own time." He gripped a teaspoon with one hand. "Where will you be tonight?"

"I don't know. I'll be somewhere else but it won't be anywhere I've chosen because I'm not going to choose anything."

Mr. Allingham put the knotted teaspoon down.

"What do you want, Samuel?" he whispered.

"I don't know." Samuel touched his breast pocket where his wallet was. "I know I want to find Lucille Harris," he said.

"Who's Lucille Harris?"

Then Mr. Allingham looked at him.

"He doesn't know," he said. "Oh, he doesn't know!"

A man and a woman sat down at the next table.

"But you promised you'd destroy him," the woman said.

"I'll do it, I'll do it," the man said. "Don't you worry. You drink your tea. Don't you worry."

They had lived a long time together, and had grown to resemble one another with their dry, bunched faces and their nibbling mouths. The woman scratched herself as she drank, as she gripped the edge of the cup with her grey lips and shook it.

"Twopence she's got a tail," Samuel said in a low voice, but Mr. Allingham had not noticed them arrive.

"That's right," he said. "You have it your own way. And she's covered all over with fur."

Samuel put his little finger in the neck of the empty bottle.

"I resign myself," Mr. Allingham said.

"But you don't understand, Mr. Allingham."

"I understand enough," he said loudly. The couple at the next table stopped talking. "You don't want to make things happen, don't you? I'll make them happen all right. You can't come in here and talk to me like you've been talking. Lucille Harris. Lucy da monk!"

The man and the woman began whispering. "And it's only half-past one," the woman said. She shook her cup like a rat.

"Come on. We're going." Mr. Allingham scraped back his chair.

"Where to?"

"Never you mind. It's I'm making things happen, isn't it?"

"I can't get my finger out of the bottle," Samuel said.

Mr. Allingham lifted up the suitcases and stood up. "What's a little bottle?" he said. "Bring it with you, son."

"Father and son, too," the woman said as Samuel followed him out.

The bottle hung heavily on his finger.

"Where now?" Outside in the roaring station.

"You follow me. And put your hand in your pocket. It looks silly."

As they walked up the slope to the street, Mr. Allingham said, "I've never been with anybody with a bottle on his finger before. Nobody else has ever had a bottle on his finger. What'd you want to put your finger in the bottle for?"

"I just pushed it in. I'll be able to get it off with soap, there's no need to make a fuss."

"Nobody else has ever had to get a bottle off with soap, that's all I'm saying. This is Praed Street."

"It's dull, isn't it?"

"All the horses have gone away," Mr. Allingham said. "This is my street. This is Sewell Street. It's dull, isn't it?"

"It's like the streets at home."

A boy passed them and shouted "Ikey Mo" to Mr. Allingham.

"This is 23. See? There's the sign, 23."

Mr. Allingham opened the front door with a key. "Second floor, first on the right."

He gave three knocks. "Mr. Allingham," he said, and they walked in.

The room was full of furniture.

# II

## *Plenty of Furniture*

### I

EVERY INCH of the room was covered with furniture. Chairs stood on couches that lay on tables; mirrors nearly the height of the door were propped, back to back, against the walls, reflecting and making endless the hills of desks and chairs with their legs in the air, sideboards, dressing tables, chests-of-drawers, more mirrors, empty bookcases, washbasins, clothes cupboards. There was a double bed, carefully made, with the ends of the sheets turned back, lying on top of a dining table on top of another table; there were electric lamps and lampshades, trays and vases, lavatory bowls and basins, heaped in the armchairs that stood on cupboards and tables and beds, touching the ceiling. The one window, looking out on the road, could just be seen through the curved legs of sideboards on their backs. The walls behind the standing mirrors were thick with pictures and picture frames.

Mr. Allingham climbed into the room over a stack of mattresses, then disappeared.

"Hop in, boy." His voice came up from behind a high kitchen dresser hung with carpets; and, climbing over, Samuel looked down to see him seated on a chair on a couch, leaning back comfortably, his elbow on the shoulder of a statue.

"It's a pity we can't cook here," Mr. Allingham said. "There's plenty of stoves, too. That's a meat-safe," he said, pointing to one corner. "Just under the bedroom suite."

"Have you got a piano?"

"There used to be one," he said. "I think it's in the other room. She put a carpet over it. Can you play?"

"I can vamp. You can tell what tunes I'm doing, easily. Is the other room like this?"

"Two more rooms, but I think the piano's locked. Yes, there's plenty of furniture," Mr. Allingham said, looking round with distaste. "Whenever I say 'That's enough now,' in she comes with her 'Plenty more room, plenty more room.' She'll find she can't get in one day, that's what'll happen. Or she can't get out; I don't know which would be the worst. It gets you sometimes you know," he said, "all this furniture."

"Is she your wife, Mr. Allingham?"

"She'll find there's a limit to everything. You get to feel kind of trapped."

"Do you sleep here?"

"Up there. It's nearly twelve foot high. I've measured. I can touch the ceiling when I wake up."

"I like this room," Samuel said. "I think it's perhaps the best room I've ever seen."

"That's why I brought you. I thought you'd like it. Proper little den for a man with a bottle on his finger, isn't it? I told you, you're not like anybody else. Nobody else can bear the sight of it. Got your cases safe?"

"They're there. In the bath."

"You keep your eye on them, that's all. I've lost a sofa. One more suite and I'll lose my bed. And what happens when a customer comes? I'll tell you. He takes one peek through the door and off he trots. You can only buy what's on the top at the moment, see."

"Can you get into the other rooms?"

"You can," Mr. Allingham said. "She takes a dive in, head-first. I've lost all interest in the other rooms, myself. You could live and die in there and nobody'd know. There's some nice Chippendale, too. Up by the skylight."

He rested his other elbow on a hallstand.

"I got to feel lost," he said. "That's why I go

down to the buffet; there's only tables and chairs there."

Samuel sat on his perch, swinging the bottle and drumming his feet against the side of a bath mounted yards above the floor of mattresses. A carpet behind him, laid out flat and wide along the air, having no visible support, bore a great earthenware jar dangerously upon the backs of its patterned birds. High over his head, in the tall room, a rocking-chair balanced on a card-table, and the table's thin legs rested on the top of a cupboard standing up straight among pillows and fenders, with its mirrored door wide open.

"Aren't you frightened of things falling? Look at that rocking-chair. One little prod and over she comes."

"Don't you dare. Of course I'm frightened," Mr. Allingham said. "If you open a drawer over there, a wash-stand falls down over here. You've got to be quick as a snake. There's nothing on the top you'd like to buy, is there?"

"I like a lot of the things, but I haven't any money."

"No, no, you wouldn't have money. That's right. Other people have money."

"I like the big jar. You could hide a man in that. Have you got any soap for my finger?"

"Of course there's no soap, there's only wash-basins. You can't have a bath, either, and there's five baths. Why do you want a jar big enough to hide a man in? Nobody I've ever met wants to hide a man in a jar. Everybody else says that jar's too big for anything. Why do you want to find Lucille Harris, Sam?"

"I didn't mean I wanted to hide a man in it. I mean that you could if you wanted to. Oh, a man I know told me about Lucille, Mr. Allingham. I don't know why I want to find her, but that's the only London address I kept. I put the others down the lavatory in the train. When the train was moving."

"Good, good." Mr. Allingham put his hand on the thick, white neck of the naked statue, and tightened his fingers.

The door opened on to the landing. Two people came in, and climbed up the mattresses without a word. The first, a fat, short woman with black hair and a Spanish comb, who had painted her face as though it were a wall, took a sudden dive toward the corner behind Samuel and disappeared between two columns of chairs. She must have landed on cushions or a bed, for she made no sound. The second visitor was a tall, youngish man with a fixed smile; his teeth were large, like a horse's, but very white; his glistening fair hair was done in tight curls, and it smelt across the room. He stood on a spring mattress just inside the door, bouncing up and down. "Come on, Rose, don't be sulky," he said. "I know where you've gone." Then, pretending to see Samuel for the first time, "Good gracious you look like a bird up there," he said. "Is Donald hiding anywhere?"

"I'm not hiding," Mr. Allingham said. "I'm by the statue. Sam Bennet, George Ring."

George Ring bowed and bounced, rising a foot from the mattress.

He and Mr. Allingham could not see each other. Nobody could see the woman with the Spanish comb.

"I hope you've excused the room to Mr. Bennet," George Ring said. He bounced a few steps in the direction of the hidden statue.

"I don't think it needs any excusing, Mr. Ring," Samuel said. "I've never seen such a comfortable room."

"Oh, but it's terrible." George Ring was moving up and down rapidly now. "It's very kind of you to say it's comfortable, but look at the confusion. Just think of living here. You've got something on your finger, did you know that? Three guesses. It's a bottle." He shook his curls and laughed as he bounced.

"You don't know anything yet," said Mr. Allingham's voice. The heavy bouncing had shaken
down a carpet on to the hallstand and he was hidden as though in another, lower room. "You don't
know anything about him. You wait. What are you
bouncing for, George? People don't go bouncing
about like a ball as soon as they come into a room."

"What don't I know about you?" In one leap
George Ring was standing directly below Samuel,
craning up his curls.

"He doesn't know where he's going, for one
thing. And he's looking for a girl he doesn't know
called Lucille."

"Why are you looking for her?" George Ring's
head touched the bath. "Did you see her picture
in the paper?"

"No, I don't know anything about her, but I
want to see her because she's the only person I
know by name in London."

"Now you know two more, don't you? Are you
sure you don't love her?"

"Of course I'm sure."

"I thought perhaps she might be a sort of Holy
Grail. You know what I mean. A sort of ideal."

"Go on, you big pussycat," Mr. Allingham said.
"Get me out of here."

"Is this the first time you've come to London?

I felt like that when I came up first, too. Years and
years ago. I felt there was something I must find,
I can't explain it. Something just round the corner. I searched and searched. I was so innocent.
I felt like a sort of knight."

"Get me out of here," Mr. Allingham said. "I
feel like the whole room's on top of me."

"I never found it." George Ring laughed and
sighed and stroked the side of the bath. "Perhaps
you'll be lucky," he said. "You'll walk round the
corner and there she'll be. Lucille. Lucille. Is
she on the telephone?"

"Yes. I've got her number in my book."

"Oh, that makes it easier, doesn't it. Come on,
Rose," he said. "I know exactly where you are.
She's in a pet."

Samuel rocked softly on his box in the middle of
the furniture. This was the fullest room in Eng-
land. How many hundreds of houses had been
spilt in here, tables and chairs coming in on a wood-
en flood, chests and cupboards soaring on ropes
through the window and settling down like birds.
The other rooms, beyond that jostled door, would
be taller and darker even than this, with the mute,
black shape of the locked piano mountainous under
a shroud of carpets and Rose, with her comb like
the prow of a ship, driving into their darkness and

lying all night motionless and silent where she struck. Now she was dead still on a sunk bed between the column of chairs, buried alive, soft and fat and lost in a grave in a house.

"I'm going to buy a hammock," George Ring said. "I can't bear sleeping under all this furniture."

Perhaps the room was crowded at night with people who could not see each other, stretched under chairs, under sofas, dizzily asleep on the tops of raised tables, waking up every morning and crying out, "Earthquake, earthquake!"

"And then I'll go to bed like a sailor."

"Tell Rose to come and get me out of here," Mr. Allingham said, behind the cloaked hallstand, "I want to eat."

"She's sulking Donald. She's mad about a Japanese screen now."

"Do you hear that, Sam? Isn't there enough privacy in this room? Anybody can do anything, nobody can see you. I want to eat. I want to have a snack at Dacey's. Are you sleeping here to-night?"

"Who?" Samuel asked. "Me?"

"You can doss down in one of the other rooms, if you think you can get up again. There's enough beds for a harem."

"Harem," George Ring said, pronouncing it another way. "You've got company, Rose darling. Do come out and be introduced."

"Thank you, Mr. Allingham," Samuel said.

"Didn't you really have any idea at all?" George Ring bounced, and for a moment his scented head was level with Samuel's. One wide, bright, horse-toothed smile, and the head was gone. "About sleeping and things. I think it's awfully brave. You might have fallen in with all kinds of people. 'He fell among thieves.' Do you know Sir Henry Newbolt's poem?"

"He flung his empty revolver down the slope," Samuel said.

The day was moving carelessly on to a promised end and in a dark room full of furniture where he'd lie down with his bunch of wives in a crow's-nest bed or rock them in a hammock under the ceiling.

"Goodie goodie! It's so exciting to find some-one who knows about poetry. 'The voices faded and the hills slept.' Isn't that beautiful? The voices faded . . . ? I can read poetry for hours, can't I, Donald? I don't care what kind of poetry it is, I love it all. Do you know, 'Is there anybody there, said the traveller?' Where do you put the emphasis, Mr. Bennet? Can I call you Sam? Do you say, 'Is there *anybody* there' or 'Is there anybody *there*'?"

"It isn't natural," Mr. Allingham said, "for a man not to be able to see anybody when he's sitting right next to them. I'm not grumbling, but I can't see anything, that's all. It's like not being in the room."

"Oh, do be quiet, Donald. Sam and I are having a perfectly serious discussion. Of course you're in the room, don't be morbid."

"I think I'd put about the same emphasis on all the words," Samuel said.

"But don't you find it tends to make the line rather flat? '*Is* there anybody there, said the traveller,' " George Ring murmured, pacing the mattresses, his head on one side. "I feel you do want a stress somewhere."

Will I be alone tonight in the room with the piano? Samuel wondered. Alone like a man in a warehouse, lying on each bed in turn, opening cupboards and putting my hand in, looking at myself in mirrors in the dark.

"Don't you call me morbid, George Ring," Mr. Allingham said. He tried to move, but the statue fell against his chair. "I remember once I drank forty-nine Guinnesses straight off and I came home on the top of a bus. There's nothing morbid about a man who can do that. Right on the top of the bus, too, not just in the upper deck."

Or will the room be full as a cemetery, but with the invisible dead breathing and snoring all around me, making love in the cupboards, drunk as tailors in the dry baths? Suddenly a warm body might dive in through the door and lie in my bed all night without a name or a word.

"I think forty-nine Guinnesses is piggish," said George Ring.

"It was raining," Mr. Allingham said, "and I never get truculent. I may sing and I may have a bit of a dance, but I never get nasty. Give me a hand, Sam."

Samuel took the carpet off the hallstand and pushed the statue away. It had fallen between Mr. Allingham's legs. He came up slowly into sight and rubbed his eyes like a man waking.

"I told you," he said, "you get trapped. Coming to Dacey's, George?"

"I'll have to stay for hours, you know that," George Ring said. "You know I'm the only person who can humour Rosie when she's in one of her states. Oh, come on, Rosie, don't be temperamental. It's ninety per cent temper and ten per cent mental. Just because you're an actress you think you can stay under the furniture all the afternoon. I'll count five . . ."

Samuel followed Mr. Allingham to the door.

"Five, six, seven," George Ring said, as Mr. Allingham slammed the door hard, and his voice was lost in the noise of furniture falling. They went down the stairs into the hallway that smelt of cabbage, and out on to the grey street.

"I think it must have been the rocking-chair," Samuel said.

"Mrs. Dacey's is just round the corner," Mr. Allingham said. "There you are. See the Cadbury sign?"

2

Mrs. Dacey's front window was whitewashed from inside, and the words "High Class" had been scrawled across it. " 'Susan Dacey, licensed to sell tobacco,' " Samuel read aloud. "Is it a restaurant too?"

"You must tell her that," Mr. Allingham said, opening the door. A bell rang. "It hasn't been called that before." He held his foot against the door so that the bell kept ringing. "She's a woman in a thousand."

A tall, thin, dignified woman came through the private door at the back of the shop, her hands clasped in front of her. She was dressed in black almost down to the ankles, with a severe white collar, and she held her head primly as though it might spill. God help the other nine hundred and ninety-nine. But she smiled then, and her eyes were sharp and light; the dullness raced from her mouth, leaving it cruel and happy.

"Take your trotter off the door," she said.

The bell stopped.

"That's better. You made enough noise to wake the dead." She was a well-spoken woman, clear and precise, like a schoolmistress.

"Keeping well, Mrs. Dacey? This is a new friend, Sam Bennet. Two pies and two coffees, please. Where's Polly?"

"Up to no good," said Mrs. Dacey, stepping behind the counter. Her grand dress floated around her. "You're from the country," she said, over her shoulder, as she turned the coffee tap on the brass urn. "How did you find Ikey Mo?"

"That's me." Mr. Allingham blushed on one side of his face.

"I'm not from the country really." Samuel told her where he came from. "I met Mr. Allingham in the station. I'm going to sleep in his flat tonight."

"I'd sooner sleep in an ashpit," she said.

The coffee was thick and white and tasteless. They took their cups to a cubicle and Samuel brushed off the crumbs from his chair with his sleeve. His hat was gone. There were small pellets of dirt in the dust at his feet.

"You've got a bottle on your finger," she said.

"There, you see, everybody notices. Why don't you take it off, Sam? It isn't a decoration, it isn't useful, it's just a bottle."

"I think my finger must have swollen, Mr. Allingham. The bottle's much tighter now."

"Let me have a look at you again." Mrs. Dacey put on a pair of spectacles with steel rims and a hanging chain. "He's only a baby."

"I'm twenty."

"Ikey Mo, the baby farmer." She walked carefully to the back of the shop and called, "Polly, come down here. Polly. Polly."

A girl's voice called back from high up the house, "What for, ma?"

"Come and get a gentleman's bottle off."

"It sounds like a Russian composer, doesn't it, darling?" George Ring said, at the door. "What a marvellous dress, you look like a murderess."

He sat down next to Samuel.

"I couldn't get Rose to move. She's going to lie

there all day in a tantrum. Do tell me what's happening, everybody."

"It's that bottle again," Mr. Allingham said. "Why didn't he put his finger in a glass or something? I don't know what he was poking his finger about for in the first place. It's an enigma to me."

"Everything's an enigma to you. You can't understand the slightest touch of originality. I think it must be awful not to have any imagination. It's like a sense of humour."

"I'm just saying that not to be able to go in and buy a bottle of Bass without having to leave with the bottle on your finger seems to me like a kind of nightmare. That's all I'm saying."

Samuel heard Mrs. Dacey's daughter running downstairs. Then he saw her hand on the edge of the door. In the second she took to push the door open and come in, he made her a hundred faces; he made her talk and walk in all the disguises of his loves at night; he gave her golden hair, black hair, he knew that she would be gypsy-skinned and white as milk. Polly come and put the kettle on with your white, slender, brown, broad hands, and see me waiting like a grenadier or a caliph in the mousey cubicle.

"It's like one of those nightmares when you're

playing billiards and the cue's made of elastic," Mr. Allingham said.

In came a girl with a long, pale face and glasses. Her hair was not any of Samuel's colours, but only dark and dull.

"Go and help to pull his bottle off," said Mrs. Dacey.

Polly sat down on the table and took his hand. "Does it hurt? I've never done it before." She pulled at his finger.

"I hope you won't ever have to do it again, either," Mr. Allingham said. "I don't care if I haven't got any imagination. I'm glad I'm like I am without anything on my finger."

Polly bent over Samuel's hand and he saw down her dress. She knew that he was looking, but she did not start back or spread her hand across the neck of her dress; she raised her head and stared at his eyes. I shall always remember this, he said to himself. In 1933 a girl was pulling at a bottle on the little finger of my left hand while I looked down her dress. It will last longer than all my poems and troubles.

"I can't get it off," she said.

"Take him up to the bathroom then and put some soap on it," said Mrs. Dacey, in her dry, neat voice. "And mind it's only his bottle."

George Ring said as they got up to go, "Scream if you want me, I'll be up in a wink. She's the most terrible person, aren't you, darling? You wouldn't catch little George going up there all alone."

Polly led the way upstairs.

"I'm not complaining," Mr. Allingham said, "I'm just making a statement. I'm not saying it isn't all as it should be. He's got a bottle on his finger and I've got a tooth in my pie."

His voice faded.


3


SOMEONE HAD drawn the ragged curtains in the bathroom to shut out the damp old day, and the bath was half full of water with a rubber duck floating on it. As Polly closed and locked the door birds began to sing.

"It's only the birds," she said. She put the key down her dress. "You needn't be frightened."

Two cages hung from the ceiling.

But Samuel had looked frightened when she turned the key and put it away where he never wanted to find it, not when the room grew suddenly like a wood in the tangled shadows of the green curtains.

"It's a funny place to have birds," he said.

"They're mine." Polly let the hot water run and the birds sang more loudly as though they heard a waterfall. "Mr. Allingham comes here for a bath on Wednesdays and he says they sneer at him and blow little raspberries all the time he's washing. But I don't think he washes very much. Doesn't Mr. Allingham make you laugh too?"

He expected her to be smiling when she turned to him, but her face was still and grave, and all at once he saw that she was prettier than any of the girls he had made up in his mind before she opened the door downstairs. He distrusted her prettiness because of the key. He remembered what Mrs. Dacey had said when Mr. Allingham asked where Polly was. "Up to no good." He did not think she was going to put her arms around him. That would have been different. If she tried to put his head under the water he'd shout for George Ring and up he'd come like a horse, neighing and smelling of scent.

"I only locked the door because I don't want George Ring to come in. He's queer. He puts scent all over his underclothes; did you know that?

The Passing Cloud, that's what we call him. The Passing Cloud."

"You didn't have to put the key where you put it, though," Samuel said. "I might push you down and fish for it, I might be that sort."

"I don't care."

If only she would have smiled at him when she said that. But she looked as though she really did not care whether he pushed her down or whether he sat on the edge of the bath and touched the duck with his bottle.

The duck floated in circles on the used, greasy water.

"What's your name?"

"Sam."

"Mine's Mary. But they call me Polly for short."

"It isn't much shorter, is it?"

"No, it's exactly the same length."

She sat by his side on the edge of the bath. He could not think of anything to say. Here was the locked door he had often made up in stories and in his head, in bed in Mortimer Street, and the warm, hidden key, and the girl who was willing for anything. The bathroom should be a bedroom and she should not be wearing glasses.

"Will you take off your glasses, Polly?"

"If you like. But I won't be able to see very far."

"You don't have to see very far, it's only a little room," he said. "Can you see me?"

"Of course I can. You're right next to me. Do you like me better now?"

"You're very pretty, I suppose, Polly."

"Pretty Polly," she said, without a smile.

Well, he said to himself, here you are, here she is without any glasses on.

"Nothing ever happens in Sewell Street." She took his hand and let his finger with the bottle on it lie in her lap.

Here you are, he said, with your hand in her lap.

"Nothing ever happens where I come from, either. I think things must be happening everywhere except where one is. All kinds of things happen to other people. So they say," he said.

"The man who was lodging next door but one cut his throat like this," she said, "before breakfast."

On his first free days since he was born Samuel sat with a loose girl in a locked bathroom over a tea-shop, the dirty curtains were drawn, and his hand lay on her thighs. He did not feel any emotion at all. O God, he thought, make me feel something, make me feel as I ought to, here is something happening and I'm cool and dull as a man in a bus. Make me remember all the stories. I caught her in my arms, my heart beat against hers, her body was trembling, her mouth opened like a flower. The lotus of Osiris was opening to the sun.

"Listen to the old birds," she said, and he saw that the hot water was running over the rim of the washbasin.

I must be impotent, he thought.

"Why did he cut his throat like that, Polly? Was it love? I think if I was crossed in love I'd drink brandy and whisky and crème de menthe and that stuff that's made with eggs."

"It wasn't love with Mr. Shaw. I don't know why he did it. Mrs. Bentley said there was blood everywhere, everywhere, and all over the clock. He left a little note in the letter-rack and all it said was that he'd been meaning to do it ever since October. Look, the water'll drip right through into the kitchen."

He turned it off. The birds stopped singing.

"Perhaps it was love, really. Perhaps he loved you, Polly, but he wouldn't say so. From a distance."

"Go on, he had a limp," she said. "Old Dot and Carry. How old are you?"

"Twenty."

"No, you're not."

"Well, nearly."

"No you're not."

Then they were silent, sitting on the bath, his hand in her lap. She trailed her pale hand in the water. The birds began again.

"Pale hands I love," he said.

"Beside the Shalimar. Do you, Sam? Do you love my hands? That's a funny thing to say." She looked dully at the long, floating weed in the water and made a wave. "It's like the evening here."

"It's like evening in the country," he said. "Birds singing and water. We're sitting on a bank by the river now."

"Having a picnic."

"And then we're going to take our clothes off and have a swim. Gee, it'll be cold. You'll be able to feel all the fish swimming about."

"I can hear the 47 bus, too," she said. "People are going home to tea. It's cold without any clothes on, isn't it? Feel my arm, it's like snow, only not so white. Pale hands I love," she began to sing. "Do you love me altogether?"

"I don't know. I don't think I feel anything like that at all. I never do feel much until afterwards and then it's too late."

"Now it isn't too late. It isn't too late, Sam.

We're alone. Polly and Sam. I'll come and have a swim with you if you like. In the dirty old river with the duck."

"Don't you ever smile, Polly? I haven't seen you smile once."

"You've only known me for twenty minutes. I don't like smiling much, I think I look best when I'm serious, like this." She saddened her eyes and mouth. "I'm a tragedienne. I'm crying because my lover's dead."

Slowly tears came to her eyes.

"His name was Sam and he had green eyes and brown hair. He was ever so short. Darling, darling, darling Sam, he's dead." The tears ran down her cheeks.

"Stop crying now, Polly. Please. Stop crying. You'll hurt yourself."

But she was crying pitifully.

"Stop it, Polly, pretty Polly." He put his arm round her shoulders. He kissed her on the cheek. It was warm and wet. "Nobody's dead, Polly darling," he said. She cried and moaned his name in the abandon of her made grief, tore at the loose, low neck of her dress, threw back her hair and raised her damp eyes to the birds in their cages and the cracked heavens of the ceiling.

"You're doing it fine," he said in despair, shak-

ing her shoulders. "I've never seen such fine crying. Stop now, please, Polly, please, while you can
stop."

Ninety-eight per cent of the human body is
water, he thought. Polly Dacey is all salt water.
She sat by his side like a flood in an apron.

"I'll do anything you like if you'll only stop,"
he said. "You'll drown yourself, Polly. I'll promise to do anything in the world."

She dried her eyes on her bare arm.

"I wasn't really breaking my heart, silly. I was
only depicting. What'll you do, then? Anything?
I can depict being glad because my lover's not
really dead, too. The War Office made a mistake."

"Anything," he said. "I want to see you being
glad tomorrow. You mustn't do one after the
other."

"It's nothing to me, I can do them all in a row.
I can do childbirth and being tight and——"

"You do being quiet. Do being a quiet lady sitting on a bath, Polly."

"I will if you'll come and have a swim with me.
You promised." She patted her hair into place.

"Where?"

"In the bath. You get in first, go on. You can't
break your promise."

George Ring, he whispered, gallop upstairs now

and bite your way through the door. She wants me to sit with my overcoat on and my bottle on my finger in the cold, greasy bath, in the half-dark bathroom, under the sneering birds.

"I've got a new suit," he said.

"Take it off, silly. I don't want you to go in the bath with your clothes on. Look, I'll put something over the window so you can undress in the dark. Then I'll undress too. I'll come in the bath with you. Sam, are you frightened?"

"I don't know. Couldn't we take our clothes off and not go in the bath? I mean, if we want to take them off at all. Someone might come in. It's terribly cold, Polly. Terribly cold."

"You're frightened. You're frightened to lie in the water with me. You won't be cold for long."

"But there's no sense in it. I don't want to go in the bath. Let's sit here and you do being glad, Polly."

He could not move his hand, she had caught the bottle between her legs.

"You don't want to be frightened. I'm not any older than you are," she said, and her whispering mouth was close to his ear. "As soon as you get in the bath I'll jump on top of you in the dark. You can pretend I'm somebody you love if you don't

like me properly. You can call me any name." She
dug her nails into his hand. "Give me your coat,
I'll hang it over the window. Dark as midnight,"
she said, as she hung the coat up, and her face in
the green light through the curtains was like a
girl's under the sea. Then all the green went out,
and he heard her fumbling. I do not want to
drown. I do not want to drown in Sewell Street off
Circe Street, he whispered under his breath.

"Are you undressing? I can't hear you. Quick,
quick, Sam."

He took off his jacket and pulled his shirt over
his head. Take a good look in the dark, Mortimer
Street, have a peek at me in London.

"I'm cold," he said.

"I'll make you warm, beautifully warm, Sam."
He could not tell where she was, but she was moving in the dark and clinking a glass. "I'm going to
give you some brandy. There's brandy, darling, in
the medicine cupboard. I'll give you a big glass.
You must drink it right down."

Naked, he slipped one leg over the edge of the
bath and touched the icy water.

Come and have a look at impotent Samuel Bennet from Mortimer Street off Stanley's Grove
trembling to death in a cold bath in the dark near
Paddington Station. I am lost in the metropolis

with a rubber duck and a girl I cannot see pouring brandy into a tooth-glass. The birds are going mad in the dark. It's been such a short day for them, Polly.

"I'm in the bath now."

"I'm undressing too. Can you hear me?" she said softly. "That's my dress rustling. Now I'm taking my petticoat off. Now I'm naked." A cold hand touched him on the face. "Here's the brandy, Sam. Sam, my dear, drink it up and then I'll climb in with you. I'll love you, Sam, I'll love you up. Drink it all up, then you can touch me."

He felt the glass in his hand and he lifted it up and drank all that was in it.

"Christ!" he said in a clear, ordinary voice. "Christ!"

Then the birds flew down and kicked him on the head, carefully between the eyes, brutally on each temple, and he fell back in the bath.

That was all the birds singing under the water, and the sea was full of feathers that swam up his nostrils and into his mouth. A duck as big as a ship sailed up on a drop of water as big as a house and smelt his breath as it spurted out from broken, bleeding lips, like flames and waterspouts. Here came a wave of brandy and birds, and Mr. Allingham, naked as a baby, riding on the top with his

birthmark like a rainbow, and George Ring swimming breast-stroke through the open door, and
three Mrs. Daceys gliding in yards above the
flowing ground.

The darkness drowned in a bright ball of light,
and the birds stopped.

4

VOICES BEGAN to reach him from a great distance,
travelling in lavatories in racing trains along a
liquid track, diving from the immeasurably high
ceiling into the cold sea in the enormous bath.

"Do you see what I see?" That was the voice of
the man called Allingham, who slept under the
furniture. "He's taking a little dip."

"Don't let me look, Donald, he's bare all over."
I know him, Samuel thought. That's George Ring
the horse. "And he's ill too. Silly Sam."

"Lucky Sam. He's drunk, George. Well, well,
well, and he hasn't even got his bottle off. Where's
Polly?"

"You look over there," Mrs. Dacey said. "Over
F

there on the shelf. He's drunk all the eau de cologne."

"He must have been thirsty."

Large, bodiless hands came over the bath and lifted him out.

"He's eccentric," Mr. Allingham said, as they laid him on the floor, "that's all I'm saying. I'm not preaching, I'm not condemning. I'm just saying that other people get drunk in the proper places."

The birds were singing again in the electric dawn as Samuel fell quietly to sleep.

# III

## *Four Lost Souls*

### I

HE SANK into the ragged green water for the second time and, rising naked with seaweed and a woman under each arm and a mouthful of broken shells, he saw the whole of his dead life standing trembling before him, indestructible and unsinkable, on the brandy-brown waves. It looked like a hallstand.

He opened his mouth to speak, but a warm wave rushed in.

"Tea," said Mrs. Dacey. "Tea with plenty of sugar every five minutes. That's what I always gave him, and it didn't do a bit of good."

"Not too much Worcester, George; don't bury the egg."

"I won't," Samuel said.

"Oh, listen to the birds. It's been such a short night for the birds, Polly."

"Listen to the birds," he said clearly, and a burning drink drowned his tongue.

"They've laid an egg," Mr. Allingham said.

83

"Try some Coca-Cola, Donald. It can't do any harm; he's had tea and a prairie oyster and angostura and Oxo and everything."

"I used to pour the tea down by the pint," Mrs. Dacey said affectionately, "and up it came, lump sugar and all."

"He doesn't want a Coca-Cola. Give him a drop of your hair oil. I knew a man who used to squeeze boot-blacking through a veil."

"You know everybody piggish. He's trying to sit up, the poor darling."

Samuel wrestled into the dry world and looked around a room in it, at Mrs. Dacey, now miraculously divided into one long woman, folding her black silk arms in the doorway, at George Ring arching his smile and hair toward the rusty taps, at Mr. Allingham resigned above him.

"Polly's gone," he said.

It was then that he understood why the three persons in the bathroom were so tall and far. I am on the floor, looking up, he said to himself. But the others were listening.

"You're naked too," Mr. Allingham said, "under the blanket."

"Here's a nice wet sponge." George Ring dabbed and smoothed. "Keep it on your forehead. There, like that. That better?"

"Eau de cologne is for outside the body," said Mrs. Dacey without disapproval, "and I'll give our Polly such a clip. I'll clip her on the earhole every time she opens her mouth."

Mr. Allingham nodded. "Whisky I can understand," he said. "But eau de cologne! You put that on handkerchieves. You don't put whisky on handkerchieves." He looked down at Samuel. "I don't."

"No, mustn't suck the sponge, Sam."

"I suppose he thinks red biddy's like bread and milk," Mr. Allingham said.

They gathered his clothes from the side of the bath and hurriedly dressed him. And not until he was dressed and upright, shivering along the landing to the dark stairs, did he try to speak again. George Ring and Mr. Allingham held his arms and guided him toward the top of that winding grave. Mrs. Dacey, the one mourner, followed with a rustle of silk.

"It was the brandy from the medicine cupboard," he said, and down they went into the coarse, earth-like silence of the stairs.

"Give me furniture polish," Mr. Allingham said. "Crack. Mind your head. Especially when I'm out of sorts in the bath."

The darkness was settling like more dirt and

dust over the silent shop. Someone had hung up a sign, "Closed", on the inside of the window not facing the street. "Meths is finicky," Mr. Allingham said.

They sat Samuel down on a chair behind the counter and he heard Mrs. Dacey, still on the stairs, calling for Polly up into the dark, dirty other floors and caves of the drunken house. But Polly did not answer.

She would be in her locked bedroom now, crying for Sam gone, at her window staring out on to the colourless, slowly disappearing street and the tall houses down at heel; or depicting, in the kitchen, the agony of a woman in childbirth, writhing and howling round the crowded sink; or being glad at a damp corner of the landing.

"Silly goose," said George Ring, sitting long-legged on the table and smiling at Samuel with a ferocious coyness. "You might have been drownded. Drownded," he said again, looking slyly up from under the spider line of his eyebrows.

"Lucky you left the door open," Mr. Allingham said. He lit a cigarette and looked at the match until it burned his finger. "I suppose," he said, his finger in his mouth.

"Our maid at home always said 'drownded'," said George Ring.

"But I saw Polly lock the door. She put the key down her dress." Samuel spoke with difficulty from behind the uncertain counter. The words came out in a rush, then reversed and were lost, tumbling among the sour bushes under his tongue. "She put it down her dress," he said, and paused at the end of each word to untie the next. Now the shop was almost entirely dark.

"And chimbley. You know, for chimney. Well, my dear, the door was open when we went up. No key, no Polly."

"Just a boy in the bath," Mr. Allingham said. "Do you often get like that, Sam? The water was up to your chin."

"And the dirt!"

"It wasn't my dirt. Someone had been in the bath before. It was cold," Samuel said.

"Yes, yes." Samuel could see Mr. Allingham's head nodding. "That alters the situation, doesn't it? Dear God," he said, "you should have gone in with your clothes on like everybody else."

"Polly's gone," said Mrs. Dacey. She appeared out of nowhere in the wall and stood behind the counter at Samuel's side. Her rustling dress brushed against his hands, and he drew them sharply back. I touched a funeral, he said to the dazed boy in his chair. Her corpse-cold hand fell against his cheek, chilling him out of a moment's sleep. The coffin has walked upright into my sitting bed.

"Oooh," he said aloud.

"Still cold, baby?" Mrs. Dacey bent down, creaking like a door, and mothered him about the hair and mouth.

There had been little light all day, even at dawn and noon, mostly the close, false light of bedroom and restaurant. All day he had sat in small, dark places, bathroom and travelling lavatory, a jungle of furniture, a stuffed shop where no one called except these voices saying:

"You looked so defenceless, Sam, lying there all cold and white."

"Where was Moses when the light went out, Mrs. Dacey?"

"Like one of those cherubs in the Italian Primitives, only with a bottle on your finger, of course."

"In the dark. Like this."

"What did our Polly do to you, the little tart?" Mrs. Dacey said in her tidy, lady's voice.

Mr. Allingham stood up. "I'm not listening. Don't you say a word, Sam, even if you could. No explanations. There he was, gassed in the bath, at half-past four in the afternoon. I can stand so much."

"I want to go out," Samuel said.

"Out the back?"

"Out."

Out of the blind, stripping hole in a wall, aviary and menagerie, cold water shop, into the streets without locks. I don't want to sleep with Polly in a drawer. I don't want to lie in a cellar with a wet woman, drinking polish. London is happening everywhere; let me out, let me go. Mrs. Dacey is all cold fingers.

"Out then. It's six o'clock. Can you walk, son?"

"I can walk okay; it's my head."

Mrs. Dacey, unseen, stroked his hair. Nobody can see, he said silently, but Mrs. Susan Dacey, licensed to sell tobacco, is stroking my hair with her lizards; and he gave a cry.

"I've got no sympathy," said Mr. Allingham. "Are you coming, Sue?"

"Depends where you're going."

"Taking the air down the Edgware Road. He's got to see around, hasn't he? You don't come up from the provinces to drink eau de cologne in the bath."

They all went out, and Mrs. Dacey locked the shop.

It was raining heavily.

2

"FUN!" George Ring said.

They walked out of Sewell Street into Praed Street arm-in-arm.

"I'm a fool for the rain." He shook his clinging curls and danced a few steps on the pavement.

"My new brown overcoat's in the bathroom," Samuel said, and Mrs. Dacey covered him with her umbrella.

"Go on, you're not the sort that puts a coat on in the rain, are you? Stop dancing, George."

But George Ring danced down the pavement in the flying rain and pulled the others with him; unwillingly they broke into a dancing run under the lamp posts' drizzle of light, Mrs. Dacey, black as a deacon, jumping high over the puddles with a rustle and creak, Mr. Allingham, on the outside, stamping and dodging along the gutter, Samuel gliding light and dizzy with his feet hardly touching the ground.

"Look out. People," cried Mr. Allingham, and dragged them, still dancing, out on to the slippery street. Caught in a circle of headlights and chased by horns, they stamped and scampered on to the pavement again, clinging fast to each other, their faces glistening, cold and wet.

"Where's the fire, George? Go easy, boy, go easy." But Mr. Allingham, one foot in the gutter, was hopping along like a rabbit and tugging at George Ring's arm to make him dance faster. "It's all Sam's fault," he said as he hopped, and his voice was high and loud like a boy's in the rain.

Look at London flying by me, buses and glow-worms, umbrellas and lamp posts, cigarettes and eyes under the water doorways, I am dancing with three strangers down Edgware Road in the rain, cried Samuel to the gliding boy around him. Light and without will as a suit of feathers, he held on to their arms, and the umbrella rode above them like a bird.

Cold and unsmiling, Mrs. Dacey skipped by his side, seeing nothing through her misted glasses.

And George Ring sang as he bounced, with his drenched hair rising and falling in level waves, "Here we go gathering nuts and may, Donald and Mrs. Dacey and George and Sam."

When they stopped, outside the Antelope, Mr. Allingham leaned against the wall and coughed until he cried. All the time he coughed he never removed his cigarette.

"I haven't run for forty years," he said, his shoulders shaking, and his handkerchief like a flag to his mouth. He led them into the Saloon Bar, where three young women sat with their shoes off in front of the electric log fire.

"Three whiskies. What's yours, Sam? Nice drop of Kiwi?"

"He'll have whisky, too," Mrs. Dacey said. "See, he's got his colour back."

"Kiwi's boot-polish," one of the young women whispered, and she bent, giggling, over the grate. Her big toe came out of a hole in her stocking, suddenly, like a cold inquisitive nose, and she giggled again.

This was a bar in London. Dear Peggy, Samuel wrote with his finger on the counter, I am drinking in a bar called the Antelope in Edgware Road with a furniture dealer, the proprietress of a tea-shop, three young women and George Ring. I have put these facts down clearly because the scent I drank in the bath is still troublesome and people will not keep still. I am quite well but I do not know for how long.

"What're you doing, Sam? Looks like you're drawing. I've got a proper graveyard in my chest, haven't I? Cough, cough," Mr. Allingham said, angrily between each cough.

"It wasn't the cough that carried him off," the young woman said. Her whole plump body was giggling.

Everything is very trivial, Samuel wrote. Mr. Allingham is drunk on one whisky. All his face goes pale except his mark.

"Here we are," Mr. Allingham said, "four lost souls. What a place to put a man in."

"The Antelope's charming," said George Ring. "There's some real hunting prints in the private bar." He smiled at Sam and moved his long, blunt fingers rapidly along the counter as though he were playing a piano. "I'm all rhythm. It's like a kind of current in me."

"I mean the world. This is only a little tiny bit in it. This is all right, it's got regular hours; you can draw the curtains, you know what to expect here. But look at the world. You and your currents," Mr. Allingham said.

"No, really it's rippling out of me." George Ring tap-danced with one foot and made a rhythmical, kissing noise with his tongue against the roof of his mouth.

"What a place to drop a man in. In the middle of streets and houses and traffic and people."

The young woman wagged her finger at her toe.

"You be still." Her friends were giggling now, covering their faces and peeping out at Mr. Allingham between their fingers, telling each other to go on, saying "hotcha" and "hi de ho" and "Minnie the Moocher's Wedding Day" as George Ring tapped one narrow, yellow buckskin shoe and strummed on the counter. They rolled their eyes and said, "Swing it, sister," then hissed again into a giggle.

"I've been nibbling away for fifty years now," Mr. Allingham said, "and look at me. Look at me." He took off his hat.

"There's hair," whispered the young woman with the hole in her stocking.

His hair was the colour of ferrets and thin on the crown; it stopped growing at the temples but came out again from the ears. His hat made him a deep, white wrinkle on his forehead.

"Here we are nibbling away all day and night, Mrs. Dacey. Nibble nibble." His brown teeth came over his lip. "No sense, no order, no nothing; we're all mad and nasty. Look at Sam there. There's a nice harmless boy, curly hair and big eyes and all. What's he do? Look at his bloody bottle."

"No language," said the woman behind the bar. She looked like a duchess, riding, rising and sinking slowly as she spoke, as though to the movements of a horse.

"Tantivy," Samuel said, and blushed as Mr. Allingham pointed a stained finger.

"That's right. Always the right word in the right place. Tantivy! I told you, people are all mad in the world. They don't know where they're going, they don't know why they're where they are; all they want is love and beer and sleep."

"I wouldn't say no to the first," said Mrs. Dacey. "Don't pay any attention to him," she said to the woman behind the counter, "he's a philosopher."

"Calling everybody nasty," said the woman, rising. "There's people live in glass houses." Over the hurdle she goes, thought Samuel idly, and she sank again on to the hidden saddle. She must do miles in a night, he said to his empty glass.

"People think about all kinds of other things." George Ring looked at the ceiling for a vision. "Music," he said, "and dancing." He ran his fingers along the air and danced on his toes.

"Sex," said Mr. Allingham.

"Sex, sex, sex, it's always sex with you, Donald. You must be repressed or something."

"Sex," whispered the young woman by the fire.

"Sex is all right," Mrs. Dacey said. "You leave sex alone."

"Of course I'm repressed. I've been repressed for fifty years."

"You leave sex out of it." The woman behind the counter rose in a gallop. "And religion," she said.

Over she goes, clean as a whistle, over the hedge and the water-jump.

Samuel took a pound out of his wallet and pointed to the whisky on the shelf. He could not trust himself yet to speak to the riding woman with the stuffed, enormous bosom and two long milk-white loaves for arms. His throat was still on fire; the heat of the room blazed up his nostrils into his head, and all the words at the tip of his tongue caught like petrol and gorse; he saw three young women flickering by the metal logs, and his three new friends thundered and gestured before him with the terrible exaggeration of people of flesh and blood moving like dramatic prisoners on a screen, doomed forever to enact their pettiness in a magnified exhibition.

He said to himself: Mrs. Antelope, pouring the whisky as though it were four insults, believes that sex is a bed. The act of love is an act of the bed itself; the springs cry "Tumble" and over she goes, horse and all. I can see her lying like a log on a bed, listening with hate and disgust to the masterly voice of the dented sheets.

He felt old and all-knowing and unsteady. His immediate wisdom weighed so heavily that he clutched at the edge of the counter and raised one arm, like a man trapped in the sea, to signal his sinking.

"You may," Mrs. Dacey said, and the room giggled like a girl.

Now I know, thought Samuel beneath his load, as he struggled to the surface, what is meant by a pillar of the church. Long, cold Mrs. Dacey could prop Bethesda on the remote top of her carved head and freeze with her eyes the beetle-black sinners where they scraped below her. Her joke boomed in the roof.

"You've dropped a fiver, Sam." Mr. Allingham picked up a piece of paper and held it out on the sun-stained palm of his hand.

"It's Lucille Harris's address," Samuel said.

"Why don't you give her a ring? The phone's on the stairs, up there." George Ring pointed. "Outside the Ladies."

Samuel parted a curtain and mounted.

"*Outside* the Ladies," a voice said from the sinking room.

He read the instructions above the telephone, put in two pennies, dialled, and said, "Miss Harris? I'm a friend of Austin's.

"I am a friend of nobody's. I am detached," he whispered into the buzzing receiver. "I am Lopo the outlaw, loping through the night, companion of owls and murderers. Tu wit to woo," he said aloud into the mouthpiece.

She did not answer, and he shuffled down the stairs, swung open the curtain, and entered the bright bar with a loping stride.

The three young women had gone. He looked at the grate to see if their shoes were still there, but they had gone too. People leave nothing.

"She must have been out," he said.

"We heard," said Mr. Allingham. "We heard you talking to her owl." He raised his glass and stared at it, standing sadly and savagely in the middle of the room, like a man with oblivion in his hand. Then he made his choice, and drank.

"We're going places," he said. "We're taking a taxi and Sam is going to pay for it. We're going to the West End to look for Lucille."

"I knew she was a kind of Holy Grail," George Ring said when they were all in the darkness of the taxi rattling through the rain.

Samuel felt Mrs. Dacey's hand on his knee.

"Four knights at arms, it's terribly exciting. We'll call at the Gayspot first, then the Cheerioh, then the Neptune."

"Four lost souls."

The hand ached on along the thigh, five dry fishes dying on a cloth.

"Marble Arch," Mr. Allingham said. "This is where the fairies come out in the moon."

And the hurrying crowd in the rain might have had no flesh or blood.

"Park Lane."

The crowd slid past the bonnet and the windows, mixed their faces with no features and their liquid bodies under a sudden blaze, or vanished into the streaming light of a tall door that led into the bowels of rich night London where all the women wore pearls and pricked their arms with needles.

A car backfired.

"Hear the champagne corks?"

Mr. Allingham is listening to my head, Samuel thought as he drew away from the fingers in the corner.

"Piccadilly. Come on Allingham's tour. That's the Ritz. Stop for a kipper, Sam?"

The Ritz is closed forever. All the waiters would be bellowing behind their hands. Gustave, Gustave, cried a man in an opera hat, he is using the

wrong fork.  He is wearing a tie with elastic at the
back.  And a woman in evening dress cut so low he
could see her navel with a diamond in it leaned over
his table and pulled his bow tie out and let it fly
back again to his throat.

"The filthy rich," he said.  My place is among
the beggars and the outlaws.  With power and violence Samuel Bennet destroys the whole artifice of
society in his latest novel, *In the Bowels*.

"Piccadilly Circus.  Centre of the world.  See the
man picking his nose under the lamp post?  That's
the Prime Minister."

3

THE GAYSPOT was like a coal cellar with a bar at
one end, and several coalmen were dancing with
their sacks.  Samuel, at the door, swaying between
Mrs. Dacey and George Ring, felt his thigh, still
frightened.  He did not dare look down at it in case
even the outside of the trouser-leg bore the in-
excusable imprint of his terror in the taxi.

"It's cosmopolitan," George Ring whispered. "Look at the nigger."

Samuel rubbed the night out of his eyes and saw the black men dancing with their women, twirling them among the green cane chairs, between the fruit machine and the Russian billiard table. Some of the women were white, and smoked as they danced. They pussed and spied around the room, unaware of their dancing, feeling the arms around them as though around the bodies of different women: their eyes were for the strangers entering, they went through the hot movements of the dance like women in the act of love, looking over men's shoulders at their own remote and unconniving faces in a looking-glass. The men were all teeth and bottom, flashers and shakers, with little waists and wide shoulders, in double-breasted pin-stripe and sleek, licked shoes, all ageless and unwrinkled, waiting for the flesh-pot, proud and silent and friendly and hungry—jerking round the smoking cellar under the centre of the world to the music of a drum and a piano played by two pale white cross boys whose lips were always moving.

As George Ring weaved Samuel through the dancers to the bar they passed a machine and Samuel put in a penny for a lemon. Out came one and sixpence.

"Who's going to win the Derby, Sam?" said Mr. Allingham, behind them.

"Isn't he a lucky poet?" George Ring said.

Mrs. Dacey, in half a minute, had found a partner as tall as herself and was dancing through the smoke like a chapel. He had powdered his face to hide a scar from the corner of his eye to his chin.

"Mrs. Dacey's dancing with a razor-man," Samuel said.

This was a breath and a scar of the London he had come to catch. Look at the knickerless women enamouring from the cane tables, waiting in the fumes for the country cousins to stagger in, all savings and haywisps, or the rosy-cheeked old men with buttonholes whose wives at home were as lively as bags of sprouts. And the dancing cannibal-mouthed black razor kings shaking their women's breasts and blood to the stutter of the drums, snakily tailored in the shabby sweat-smelling jungle under the wet pavement. And a crimped boy danced like a girl, and the two girls serving were as harsh as men.

Mr. Allingham bought four white wines. "Go on. He did it on a pin-table. You could bring your Auntie here, couldn't you, Monica?" he said to the girl with the bow tie pouring their drinks.

"Not my Auntie," Samuel said. Auntie Morgan Pont-Neath-Vaughan in her elastic-sided boots. "She doesn't drink," he said.

"Show Monica your bottle. He's got a bottle on his finger."

Samuel dug his hand deep in his jacket pocket. "She doesn't want to see an old bottle." His chest began to tickle as he spoke, and he slipped two fingers of his right hand between the buttons of his shirt on to his bare flesh. "No vest," he said in surprise, but the girl had turned away.

"It's a Sunday School," Mr. Allingham said. "Tasted your wine yet, Sam? This horse's unfit to work. A regular little bun dance. You could bring the vicar's wife in here."

Mrs. Cotmore-Richards, four foot one and a squeak in her stockinged trotters.

"A regular little vestry," Mr. Allingham said. "See that woman dancing? The one who fell in the flour-bin. She's a bank manager's niece."

The woman with the dead white face smiled as she passed them in the arms of a padded boy.

"Hullo, Ikey."

"Hullo, Lola. She's pretendin', see. Thinks she's Starr Faithfull."

"Is she a prostitute, Mr. Allingham?"

"She's a manicurist, Sammy. How's your

cuticles? Don't you believe everything you see, especially after it's dark. This is all pretending. Look at Casanova there with the old girls. The last time he touched a woman he had a dummy in his mouth."

Samuel turned around. George Ring whinnied in a corner with several women. Their voices shrilled and rasped through the cross noise of the drums.

"Lucy got a beating the last time I see her," said a woman with false teeth and a bald fur. "He said he was a chemist."

"Lucille," George Ring said, impatiently shaking his curls. "Lucille Harris."

"With a clothes-brush. He had it in a little bag."

"There's a chemist," said a woman wearing a picture hat.

"He doesn't mean Lucy Wakefield," another woman said.

"Lucy Wakefield's in the Feathers with a man from Crouch End," said the bank manager's niece, dancing past. The boy who danced with her was smiling with his eyes closed.

"Perhaps he got a leather belt in his little bag," said the woman with the fur.

"It's all the same in a hundred years," said the

woman in the picture hat. She went down to her white wine, widening her legs like an old mule at a pool, and came up gasping. "They put hair oil in it."

This was all wrong. They spoke like the women who wore men's caps and carried fishfrails full of empties in the Jug and Bottle of the Compasses at home.

"Keeps away the dandruff."

He did not expect that the nightclub women under the pavement should sing and twang like sirens or lure off his buttons with their dangerous, fringed violet eyes. London is not under the bedclothes where all the company is grand and vile by a flick of the cinema eye, and the warm linen doors are always open. But these women with the shabby faces and the comedians' tongues, squatting and squabbling over their mother's ruin, might have lurched in from Llanelly on a football night, on the arms of short men with leeks. The women at the tables, whom he had seen as enamouring shapes when he first came in dazed from the night, were dull as sisters, red-eyed and thick in the head with colds; they would sneeze when you kissed them or hiccup and say Manners in the dark traps of the hotel bedrooms.

"Good as gold," he said to Mr. Allingham. "I

thought you said this was a low place, like a speakeasy."       .

"Speak easy yourself. They don't like being called low down here." Mr. Allingham leant close, speaking from the side of his mouth "They're too low for that. It's a regular little hell-hole," he whispered. "It's just warming up. They take their clothes off soon and do the hula hula; you'll like that."

"Nobody knows Lucille," George Ring said. "Are you sure she isn't Lucy? There's a lovely Lucy."

"No, Lucille."

" 'She dwells beside the springs of Dove.' I think I like Wordsworth better than Walter de la Mare sometimes. Do you know 'Tintern Abbey'?"

Mrs. Dacey appeared at Samuel's shoulder. "Doesn't baby dance?" He shuddered at the cold touch of her hand on his neck. Not here. Not now. That terrible impersonal Bethesda rape of the fingers. He remembered that she had carried her umbrella even while she danced.

"I got a sister in Tintern," said a man behind them.

"Tintern Abbey." George Ring pouted and did not turn round.

"Not in the Abbey, she's a waitress."

"We were talking about a poem."

"She's not a bloody nun," the man said.

The music stopped, but the two boys on the little platform still moved their hands and lips, beating out the dance in silence.

Mr. Allingham raised his fist. "Say that again and I'll knock you down."

"I'll blow you down," the man said. He puffed up his cheeks, and blew. His breath smelt of cloves.

"Now, now." Mrs. Dacey levelled her umbrella.

"People shouldn't go around insulting nuns then," Mr. Allingham said as the ferrule tapped his waistcoat.

"I'll blow you down," the man said. "I never insulted any nun. I've never spoken to a nun."

"Now, now." The umbrella drove for his eyes, and he ducked.

"You blow again," said Mrs. Dacey politely, "I'll push it up your snout and open it."

"Don't you loathe violence," George Ring said. "I've always been a terrible pacifist. One drop of blood and I feel slimy all over. Shall we dance?"

He put his arm round Samuel's waist and danced him away from the bar. The band began again though none of the couples had stopped dancing.

"But we're two men," Samuel said. "Is this a waltz?"

"They never play waltzes here, it's just self-expression. Look, there's two other men dancing."

"I thought they were girls."

"My friend thought you were a couple of girls," George Ring said in a loud voice as they danced past them. Samuel looked at the floor, trying to follow the movements of George Ring's feet. One, two, three, turn around, tap.

One of the young men squealed, "Come up and see my Aga Cooker."

One, two, three, swirl and tap.

"What sort of a girl is Polly Dacey, really? Is she mad?"

I'm like thistledown, thought Samuel. Swirl about and swirl again, on the toes now, shake those hips.

"Not so heavy, Sam. You're like a little Jumbo. When she went to school she used to post mice in the pillar-box and they ate up all the letters. And she used to do things to boys in the scullery. I can't tell you. You could hear them screaming all over the house."

But Samuel was not listening any more. He

circled and stumbled to a rhythm of his own among the flying legs, dipped and retreated, hopped on one leg and spun, his hair falling over his eyes and his bottle swinging. He clung to George Ring's shoulder and zig-zagged away from him, then bounced up close again.

"Don't swing the bottle. Don't swing it.. Look out. Sam. Sam."

Samuel's arm flew back and a small woman went down. She grabbed at his legs and he brought George Ring with him. Another man fell, catching fast to his partner's skirt. A long rip and she tumbled among them, her legs in the air, her head in a heave of bellies and arms.

Samuel lay still. His mouth pressed on the curls at the nape of the neck of the woman who had fallen first. He put out his tongue.

"Get off my head; you've got keys in your pocket."

"Oh, my leg!"

"That's right. Easy does it. Upsadaisy."

"Someone's licking me," cried the woman at the bottom.

Then the two girls from behind the bar were standing over them, slapping and kicking, pulling them up by the hair.

"It was that one's fault. He crowned her with

a bottle. I saw him," said the bank manager's niece.

"Where'd he get the bottle from, Lola?"

The girl with the bow tie dragged Samuel up by the collar and pointed to his left hand. He tried to slip it in his pocket but a hand like a black boxing glove closed over the bottle. A large black face bent down and stared into his. He saw only the whites of the eyes and the teeth.

I don't want a cut on my face. Don't cut my lips open. They only use razors in stories. Don't let him have read any stories.

"Now, now," said Mrs. Dacey's voice. The black face jerked back as she thrust out her opened umbrella, and Samuel's hand was free.

"Throw him out, Monica."

"He was dancing like a monkey, throw him out."

"If you throw him out you can throw me out too," Mr. Allingham said from the bar. He raised his fists.

Two men walked over to him.

"Mind my glasses." He did not wear any.

They opened the door and threw him up the steps.

"Bloody nun," a voice shouted.

"Now you."

"And the old girl. Look out for her brolly, Dodie."

Samuel fell on the area step below Mr. Allingham, and Mrs. Dacey came flying after with her umbrella held high.

It was still raining heavily.

4

"Just a passing call," said Mr. Allingham. As though he were sitting indoors at a window, he put out his hand to feel the rain. Shoes slopped past on the pavement above his head. Wet trousers and stockings almost touched the brim of his hat. "Just in and out," he said. "Where's George?"

I've been bounced, Samuel thought.

"It reminds me of my old man." Mrs. Dacey's face was hidden under the umbrella, as though in a private, accompanying thunder cloud. "In and out, in and out. Just one look at him, and out he went like clockwork."

Oh, the Gayspot? Can't go there, old man.

Samuel winked seriously in the dark. Oh, carrying a cargo. Swinging a bottle around. One look at me, out I went.

"He used to carry a little book with all the places he couldn't go to and he went to them every Saturday."

Fool, fool, fool, Samuel said to himself.

The steps were suddenly lit up as the door opened for George Ring. He came out carefully and tidily, to a rush of music and voices that faded at once with the vanishing of the smoky light, and stood on Mrs. Dacey's step, his mane of curls golden against the fanlight, a god or a half-horse emerging from the underworld into the common rain.

"They're awfully cross," he said. "Mrs. Cavanagh ripped her skirt and she didn't have anything on underneath. My dear, it's like Ancient Rome down there and now she's wearing a man's trousers and he's got legs exactly like a spider's. All black and hairy. Why are you sitting in the rain?"

"It's safe," Mr. Allingham said. "It's nice and safe in the rain. It's nice and rational sitting on the steps in the rain. You can't knock a woman down with a bottle here. See the stars? That's Arcturus. That's the Great Bear. That's Sirius, see, the green one. I won't show you where Venus is.

There's some people can't enjoy themselves unless they're knocking women down and licking them on the floor. They think the evening's wasted unless they've done that. I wish I was home. I wish I was lying in bed by the ceiling. I wish I was lying under the chairs like Rosie."

"Who started to fight, anyway? Let's go round the corner to the Cheerioh."

"That was ethical."

They climbed up the street, George Ring first, then Mr. Allingham, then Samuel and Mrs. Dacey. She tucked his arm in hers.

"Don't you worry. You hold on to me. Cold? You're shivering."

"It'll be Cheerioh all right."

The Cheerioh was a bad blaze, an old hole of lights. In the dark, open a cupboard full of cast-off clothes moving in a wind from nowhere, the smell of mothballs and damp furs, and find a lamp lit, candles burning, a gramophone playing.

"No dancing for you," Mr. Allingham said. "You need space. You want the Crystal Palace."

Mrs. Dacey still held Samuel by the arm. "You're safe with me. I've taken a fancy," she said. "Once I take a fancy I never let go."

"And never trust a woman who can't get up." Mr. Allingham pointed to a woman sitting in a chair by the Speedboat pin-table. "She's trying to get up all the time." The woman made a sudden movement of her shoulders. "No, no, legs first."

"This used to be the cow-shed," George Ring said, "and there was real straw on the floor."

Mrs. Dacey never lets go. Samuel saw the fancy shining behind her glasses, and in her hard mouse-trap mouth. Her cold hand hooked him. If he struggled and ran she would catch him in a corner and open her umbrella inside his nose.

"And real cows," Mr. Allingham said.

The men and women drinking and dancing looked like the older brothers and sisters of the drinkers and dancers in the club round the corner, but no one was black. There were deep green faces, dipped in a sea dye, with painted cockles for mouths and lichenous hair, sealed on the cheeks; red and purple, slate-grey, tide-marked, rat-brown and stickily whitewashed, with violet-inked eyes or lips the colour of Stilton; pink chopped, pink lidded, pink as the belly of a newborn monkey, nicotine yellow with mustard flecked eyes, rust scraping through the bleach, black hairs axle-greased down among the peroxide; squashed fly stubbles, saltcellared necks thick with pepper powder; carrot-heads, yolk-heads, black-heads, heads bald as sweetbreads.

"All white people here," Samuel said.

"The salt of the earth," Mr. Allingham said. "The foul salt of the earth. Drunk as a pig. Ever seen a pig drunk? Ever seen a monkey dancing like a man? Look at that king of the animals. See him? The one who's eaten his lips. That one smiling. That one having his honeymoon on her feet."